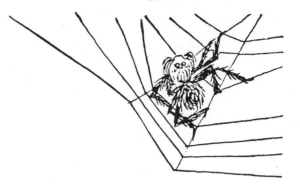

ANANSI
THE SPIDER MAN

—◦◦◦—

Jamaican Folk Tales

TOLD BY
PHILIP M. SHERLOCK

Illustrated by
MARCIA BROWN

MACMILLAN
CARIBBEAN

Macmillan Education
4 Crinan Street, London N1 9XW
A division of Macmillan Publishers Limited
Companies and representatives throughout the world

ISBN 978-0-333-35326-4

www.macmillan-caribbean.com

Printed and bound in India

2020 2019 2018
32   31   30   29

ANANSI, THE SPIDER MAN

FOR

JOHN, HILARY
AND CHRISTOPHER

CONTENTS

WHO WAS ANANSI?

He was a man and he was a spider.

When things went well he was a man, but when he was in great danger he became a spider, safe in his web high up on the ceiling. That was why his friend Mouse called him 'Ceiling Thomas.'

Anansi's home was in the villages and forests of West Africa. From there long years ago thousands of men and women came to the islands of the Caribbean. They brought with them the stories that they loved, the stories about clever Br'er Anansi, and his friends Tiger and Crow and Moos-Moos and Kisander the cat.

Today the people of the islands still tell these stories to each other. So, in some country village in Jamaica when the sun goes down the children gather round an old woman and listen to the stories of Anansi.

In the dim light they see the animals—Goat, Rat, Crow, and the others—behaving like men and women. They see how excited everyone becomes as soon as Anansi appears. They laugh at the way in which he tricks all the strong animals and gets the better of those who are much bigger than himself. At last the story comes to an end. The night and bedtime come. But next day when the children see Ceiling Thomas they know that he is more than a spider. They know that he is Anansi, the spider man, and they do him no harm.

FROM TIGER
TO ANANSI

ONCE upon a time and a long long time ago the Tiger was king
of the forest.

At evening when all the animals sat together in a circle and
talked and laughed together, Snake would ask:

'Who is the strongest of us all?'

'Tiger is strongest,' cried Dog. 'When Tiger whispers the
trees listen. When Tiger is angry and cries out, the trees
tremble.'

'And who is the weakest of all?' asked Snake.

'Anansi,' shouted Dog, and they all laughed together.
'Anansi the spider is weakest of all. When he whispers no one
listens. When he shouts everyone laughs.'

Now one day the weakest and strongest came face to face,
Anansi and Tiger. They met in a clearing of the forest. The

frogs hiding under the cool leaves saw them. The bright-green parrots in the branches heard them.

When they met, Anansi bowed so low that his forehead touched the ground. Tiger did not greet him. Tiger just looked at Anansi.

'Good morning, Tiger,' cried Anansi. 'I have a favour to ask.'

'And what is it, Anansi?' said Tiger.

'Tiger, we all know that you are strongest of us all. This is why we give your name to many things. We have Tiger lilies and Tiger stories and Tiger moths, and Tiger this and Tiger that. Everyone knows that I am weakest of all. This is why nothing bears my name. Tiger, let something be called after the weakest one so that men may know my name too.'

'Well,' said Tiger, without so much as a glance toward Anansi, 'what would you like to bear your name?'

'The stories,' cried Anansi. 'The stories that we tell in the forest evening at time when the sun goes down, the stories

about Br'er Snake and Br'er Tacumah, Br'er Cow and Br'er
Bird and all of us.'

Now Tiger liked these stories and he meant to keep them
as Tiger stories. He thought to himself, How stupid, how
weak this Anansi is. I will play a trick on him so that all the
animals will laugh at him. Tiger moved his tail slowly from
side to side and said, 'Very good, Anansi, very good. I will let
the stories be named after you, if you do what I ask.'

'Tiger, I will do what you ask.'

'Yes, I am sure you will, I am sure you will,' said Tiger,
moving his tail slowly from side to side. 'It is a little thing that
I ask. Bring me Mr. Snake alive. Do you know Snake who
lives down by the river, Mr. Anansi? Bring him to me alive
and you can have the stories.'

Tiger stopped speaking. He did not move his tail. He looked at Anansi and waited for him to speak. All the animals in the forest waited. Mr. Frog beneath the cool leaves, Mr. Parrot up in the tree, all watched Anansi. They were all ready to laugh at him.

'Tiger, I will do what you ask,' said Anansi. At these words a great wave of laughter burst from the forest. The frogs and parrots laughed. Tiger laughed loudest of all, for how could feeble Anansi catch Snake alive?

Anansi went away. He heard the forest laughing at him from every side.

That was on Monday morning. Anansi sat before his house and thought of plan after plan. At last he hit upon one that could not fail. He would build a Calaban.

On Tuesday morning Anansi built a Calaban. He took a strong vine and made a noose. He hid the vine in the grass. Inside the noose he set some of the berries that Snake loved best. Then he waited. Soon Snake came up the path. He saw the berries and went toward them. He lay across the vine and ate the berries. Anansi pulled at the vine to tighten the noose, but Snake's body was too heavy. Anansi saw that the Calaban had failed.

Wednesday came. Anansi made a deep hole in the ground. He made the sides slippery with grease. In the bottom he put

some of the bananas that Snake loved. Then he hid in the bush beside the road and waited.

Snake came crawling down the path toward the river. He was hungry and thirsty. He saw the bananas at the bottom of the hole. He saw that the sides of the hole were slippery. First he wrapped his tail tightly round the trunk of a tree, then he reached down into the hole and ate the bananas. When he was finished he pulled himself up by his tail and crawled away. Anansi had lost his bananas and he had lost Snake, too.

Thursday morning came. Anansi made a Fly Up. Inside the trap he put an egg. Snake came down the path. He was happy this morning, so happy that he lifted his head and a third of his long body from the ground. He just lowered his head, took up the egg in his mouth, and never ever touched the trap. The Fly Up could not catch Snake.

What was Anansi to do? Friday morning came. He sat and thought all day. It was no use.

Now it was Saturday morning. This was the last day. Anansi went for a walk down by the river. He passed by the hole where Snake lived. There was Snake, his body hidden in the hole, his head resting on the ground at the entrance to the hole. It was early morning. Snake was watching the sun rise above the mountains.

'Good morning, Anansi,' said Snake.

'Good morning, Snake,' said Anansi.

'Anansi, I am very angry with you. You have been trying to catch me all week. You set a Fly Up to catch me. The day before you made a Slippery Hole for me. The day before that you made a Calaban. I have a good mind to kill you, Anansi.'

'Ah, you are too clever, Snake,' said Anansi. 'You are much too clever. Yes, what you say is so. I tried to catch you, but I failed. Now I can never prove that you are the longest animal in the world, longer even than the bamboo tree.'

'Of course I am the longest of all animals,' cried Snake. 'I am much longer than the bamboo tree.'

7

'What, longer than that bamboo tree across there?' asked Anansi.

'Of course I am,' said Snake. 'Look and see.' Snake came out of the hole and stretched himself out at full length.

'Yes, you are very, very long,' said Anansi, 'but the bamboo tree is very long, too. Now that I look at you and at the bamboo tree I must say that the bamboo tree seems longer. But it's hard to say because it is further away.'

'Well, bring it nearer,' cried Snake. 'Cut it down and put it beside me. You will soon see that I am much longer.'

Anansi ran to the bamboo tree and cut it down. He placed it on the ground and cut off all its branches. Bush, bush, bush, bush! There it was, long and straight as a flagstaff.

'Now put it beside me,' said Snake.

Anansi put the long bamboo tree down on the ground beside Snake. Then he said:

'Snake, when I go up to see where your head is, you will crawl up. When I go down to see where your tail is, you will crawl down. In that way you will always seem to be longer than the bamboo tree, which really is longer than you are.'

'Tie my tail, then!' said Snake. 'Tie my tail! I know that I am longer than the bamboo, whatever you say.'

Anansi tied Snake's tail to the end of the bamboo. Then he ran up to the other end.

'Stretch, Snake, stretch, and we will see who is longer.'

A crowd of animals were gathering round. Here was something better than a race. 'Stretch, Snake, stretch,' they called.

Snake stretched as hard as he could. Anansi tied him round his middle so that he should not slip back. Now one more try. Snake knew that if he stretched hard enough he would prove to be longer than the bamboo.

Anansi ran up to him. 'Rest yourself for a little, Snake, and then stretch again. If you can stretch another six inches you will be longer than the bamboo. Try your hardest. Stretch so that you even have to shut your eyes. Ready?'

'Yes,' said Snake. Then Snake made a mighty effort. He stretched so hard that he had to squeeze his eyes shut. 'Hooray!' cried the animals. 'You are winning, Snake. Just two inches more.'

And at that moment Anansi tied Snake's head to the bamboo. There he was. At last he had caught Snake, all by himself.

The animals fell silent. Yes, there Snake was, all tied up,

ready to be taken to Tiger. And feeble Anansi had done this. They could laugh at him no more.

And never again did Tiger dare to call these stories by his name. They were Anansi stories for ever after, from that day to this.

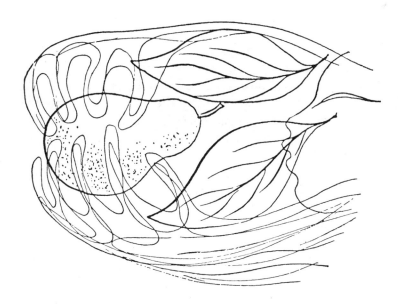

BROTHER BREEZE
AND THE PEAR TREE

ANANSI had a large pear tree in his front garden. It was a very
large tree, with wide-spreading branches and leaves of dark
green. It was not the pear tree that grows in the gardens of
northern countries. This tree bore avocado pears. The fruit
was larger than a man's fist, with a single large seed inside, and
a thick green skin. Every year the pear tree bore so heavily that
the branches almost seemed to bend beneath the weight. Then
Br'er Anansi and his family turned down their pot and stopped
cooking. They lived on bread and pears until there were no
more pears to eat.

One day it happened that Anansi was sitting under the tree
looking up at the pears that hung heavy on the tree. They were
not quite ready for picking. But they soon would be ready! He
looked up and tried to count. There were too many. As he
counted he licked his lips and wondered if perhaps even one
of the pears would be ready for picking on the following day.

But that night a strong breeze blew. Br'er Anansi became

very anxious. He knew how easy it would be for the breeze to blow the pears from the tree. The breeze blew harder and harder so that he began to fear lest it should blow the roof from the house.

By next morning, however, the breeze fell. It was very quiet outside. There was silence everywhere. Anansi opened the door and ran out into the garden. When he saw what had happened to the pear tree he began to shout and to lament. The breeze had blown all the pears off the tree. It had beaten the tree and filled the garden with leaves and with broken branches. Anansi saw that many years would pass before the pear tree recovered. Anansi's wife and children heard his shouts and ran to him. They, too, lifted up their voices and wept.

By and by, Anansi turned to his wife and said, 'Let me think—let me think! What am I going to do now?'

For a time he thought and then he said, 'I'm going to find the place where Brother Breeze lives, and I'll ask him to pay me for the pear tree!'

'Yes,' said Crooky, Anansi's wife, 'he must pay for our fine pear tree. Look at it now, with its branches torn off.' And she began to weep again.

Anansi set off. He walked a long way, and he asked many people to show him the road to the house where Breeze lived. When at last he came to the house, he stood outside for a moment, and then he knocked. A loud voice from within asked, 'Who is that?'

'It is I, Anansi, Brother Breeze.'

Breeze went to the door and said, 'Oh, it's you, Br'er Anansi, it's you. Did you know that I passed by your house the other night?'

'Yes, sir,' replied Anansi, 'but a sad accident happened when you were passing. You blew down all the fruit from my fine pear tree, and you broke off all its branches. I am sure that you did all this by mistake.'

'That is a pity, Br'er Anansi,' said Breeze. 'I am sorry to hear that. I remember now that I leaned on the tree a little heavily as I passed. I know that a pear tree is a good tree to have. Perhaps I can give you something to make up for it.'

'Thank you, Br'er Breeze,' said Anansi. 'My wife and I knew that you would help us. That pear tree was our life, you know, Mr. Breeze. It gave us all the food we needed for month after month. We turned down our pot and never had to cook when the pears were ready.'

'Well, well, Br'er Anansi, you take this instead. All you have to do with this little tablecloth that I am giving you is to spread it and ask for what you want.'

'Thank you a hundred times, a thousand times,' said Anansi. He took the little tablecloth from Breeze, folded it carefully, and set off for home.

When Anansi was half-way home he began to feel hungry, so he put down the cloth on the grass and said:

'Spread, my little tablecloth, spread.'

The tablecloth spread itself, and a big pot full of rice and peas appeared on top of it. When Anansi saw this he began to dance and sing, and he said, 'Ha-ha! Hah-ha! This is better than a pear tree, better than a pear tree that bears once a year!'

He sat down, ate all the food, folded the tablecloth, and took it home. How pleased everyone was! Anansi did not have to work, and his wife did not have to cook any more.

Then, on Monday morning, Anansi's wife went down to the river to wash the clothes. She washed the little tablecloth and spread it out on the rocks to dry. At noon she went home tired, with all the clean clothes. Br'er Anansi took the cloth and said, 'Now it's time to eat. Spread, little tablecloth, spread!'

But the little tablecloth did not spread. Anansi spoke the words again and again, but the tablecloth would not spread.

Then he said in a rage, 'It's not any good, this tablecloth.' And he went off to the house where Breeze lived. He shouted, 'Breeze, the cloth that you gave me is no good, no good at all.'

Breeze listened and scratched his head. He could not understand it. 'I don't know what can be wrong with it,' said Breeze, 'but take this pot, and when you are hungry say, "Boil, my little pot, boil!"'

Anansi hurried home with the pot. He put it down on the ground while his wife and children gathered round him. 'Boil, my little pot, boil,' he said, and they all ate the food that appeared in the little pot.

Next morning Anansi's wife looked at the pot. 'It's very dirty,' she said. 'I must wash it clean.' She washed the pot inside and outside and put it on the shelf in the kitchen.

When Br'er Anansi came home at lunch-time he put the pot on the ground and said, 'Boil, my little pot, boil!'

But nothing happened. Nothing at all. Anansi tried over and over again, but no food appeared in the pot.

Once again Anansi hurried off to the house where Breeze lived. He knocked at the door, and Breeze opened the door. 'It's Anansi again,' said Breeze to himself, 'and he is becoming a nuisance. I will have to put a stop to this.'

'Look, Breeze,' shouted Anansi, 'this is all nonsense. The pot you gave me is no good, no good at all.'

'I am sorry, Mr. Anansi,' said Breeze. 'I have one thing that might help you. Take that big stick that you see leaning up in the corner. When you want anything say, "Round about, club out, round about!"'

'Thank you, Breeze,' said Anansi, 'and I hope that this will work.'

'Yes, it will work,' said Breeze, as he closed the door and smiled to himself.

Half-way home Anansi began to feel hungry. He put the stick on the ground and said, 'Round about, club out, round about.'

The stick jumped up from the ground and began to beat Anansi, who ran and shouted, 'No round about, no club out, no round about!'

But wherever he ran the stick followed him. When he reached his home the stick began to beat his wife and children, too, until at last they ran out of the house into the river. Then the stick lay down quietly on the bank. Every time they tried to come out of the river the stick jumped up again. So they had to cross the river and go far away to the other side of the forest.

ANANSI AND
THE OLD HAG

Br'er Anansi had been wondering for a long time how to lay
his hands on some of the goats and pigs and hens and vege-
tables that belonged to his neighbours. He himself had nothing.
He turned it over in his mind for a long time until at last he
hit upon a plan.

Saturday was market day; and so, early in the morning,
Anansi set off for the market. When he got there the first
person that he met was Tiger, who said:

'Brother Anansi, for this long time I have not seen you. How are you?'

Anansi looked miserable and replied: 'Very well, thank you, Br'er Tiger.'

'But you don't look so well,' said Tiger. 'What is the matter?'

'Ah, Br'er Tiger,' said Anansi, 'last night I had a very bad dream. I dreamed that the Old Hag came to me and said that she was coming to trouble all the people in this district if they did not stop talking badly about their neighbours. It was a true dream, Br'er Tiger, and I am worried because I do not know if I should warn my friends about it.'

When Tiger heard this his face fell. This was terrible. Everyone in the forest feared the Old Hag who came riding on a broomstick by night. Sharp teeth and claws could not keep her away. Tiger remembered how a village not far off had been troubled by the Old Hag for so long that everyone had moved away, leaving the gardens and houses as they were.

'Brother Anansi,' said Tiger, 'this is serious. You had better call the people together and tell them about the dream.'

Tiger called the people, and Anansi stood up and told them all about his dream. They, too, were terrified. They could almost feel the shadow of the Old Hag falling upon them. They packed up their things quickly and hurried home before they could start quarrelling or speaking ill of each other. Br'er Anansi went home, too, well pleased with what he had done. He let a few days pass by and then took his hoe and set off down the road.

Anansi looked for the worst piece of land that he could find near the road. It was so rocky and so full of stones that nothing but thorn bushes could grow on it. He sat down in the shade of a large thorn tree and waited for someone to pass. As soon as he heard footsteps coming down the road he sprang to his feet, swung his hoe over his head, and began digging with all his might.

As he dug he sang an old digging song that he had learned as a boy:

'Donkey want water,
    Hold him, Joe!
Donkey want water,
    Hold him, Joe!'

He sang so loudly that Br'er Dog, who was walking down
the road, heard his voice and stopped.

'Good morning, Brother Anansi,' he said. 'What are you
doing with all these thorn bushes and stones?'

Anansi stopped, leaned on his hoe, wiped the sweat from his
face, and said: 'Brother Dog, can't you see that I am planting
peas and corn?'

At this Brother Dog broke into a loud laugh: 'Ha-ha-ha,
Brother Anansi,' he cried, 'I never knew that you were so fool-
ish. How do you expect peas and corn to grow in that place?
Nothing has ever grown on it except thorn bushes and rocks.'

Anansi looked at Dog very very sadly, shook his head, and
said:

'I am sorry that you talk like this, Brother Dog. Do you remember the dream that I told you about at the market? Do you remember—it was about the Old Hag?'

When Brother Dog heard this he was so frightened that he could hardly say anything. 'Oh,' he said, 'I forgot, I forgot. What am I going to do?'

Anansi said, 'Let me consider, Brother Dog, let me consider.' Then, after a short silence, he said, 'Perhaps if you make a gift to the Old Hag, Br'er Dog, she will let you off this time. What have you that you can give?'

'Only the corn in my field,' said Br'er Dog, 'and it is not ready yet. And anyway, how will I give it to the Old Hag?'

'Never worry about that,' said Anansi, 'I'll tell the Old Hag that you are going to make her a gift, and when the corn is ready I will give it to her for you. But do not breathe a word to anyone.'

Brother Dog went on his way, and Anansi went back to the shade of the thorn tree. The next to pass by was Brother Tiger. As soon as he heard the footsteps on the road Anansi jumped up and started his hoeing and singing again. Brother Tiger heard him and stopped.

'Good morning, Brother Anansi,' he said. 'What are you doing?'

'Planting corn and peas, Brother Tiger.'

'Why, surely you can't be so stupid,' said Tiger. 'Surely you have more sense than to try to plant corn and peas in the middle of all those thorn bushes and rocks. I never thought you were so stupid!'

Just then Tiger remembered Anansi's dream. He put his hand to his mouth quickly as if to hold the words back, while Brother Anansi looked at him sadly, shook his head, and said:

'Yes, Brother Tiger, I see that you remember. What trouble there will be when all the people hear that the Old Hag is troubling Tiger because he called me a fool.'

'Well,' replied Tiger, 'maybe if I give the Old Hag a gift she will let me off; and you know, Anansi, I never really meant that you were a fool! It was only idle talk.'

'Yes, Br'er Tiger,' said Anansi, 'I think that the Old Hag will not come and trouble you if you give me two of those fine goats you have, so that I may give them to her. I am sure that if you do this she will not trouble you.'

'I shall bring two of my best goats round to you tonight,' said Tiger, 'but you must keep quiet about it and not let anyone know.' So Br'er Tiger went on his way, and Br'er Anansi sat down to wait for the next one.

Before long Goat passed, and the same thing happened. Goat promised to leave two of his best chickens at Anansi's home as a gift for the Old Hag.

After this Anansi decided that he had worked hard enough for one day, and so he went home and rested. At evening time Br'er Tiger came with the two goats. A little later Br'er Goat came with the two fowls. Anansi put the animals in the back yard; and he told his neighbours that everything was all right and that the Old Hag would take the things and give them a chance.

By the following day Anansi's back yard was full of his neighbours' animals, and he could hide them no longer. He went off to his field that was full of thistles and stones. In his yard the goats bawled, the pigs grunted, and the fowls cackled so loud that the people who passed by began to stop and listen. First one or two stopped, and then a third and fourth, all asking how Anansi had got so many things so quickly. Tiger was there and Goat, too. They all began to talk to one another, and in that way they discovered that Anansi had played the same trick on each of them. Then they were angry. At last Brother Turkey said:

'I think I know how to catch Anansi, and if I catch him I will make him give back to every one of you the things he took away.'

The next day Brother Turkey went down the road to the place where Anansi was working. He whistled as he went, since his footsteps could hardly be heard. When he came to where he could see Anansi he turned his head the other way and pretended not to see him. This made Anansi sing louder than ever.

> 'Come bring my half-a-hoe
> and give it to me, oh!
> Come bring my half-a-hoe
> and give it to me, oh!'

But Turkey only whistled and took no notice of him. Then Anansi threw down his hoe and shouted: 'Hi, Brother Turkey!'

Turkey turned and looked at Anansi in surprise and said: 'Why, it's Brother Anansi. I was in such a hurry that I nearly passed without noticing you.'

'Why are you in such a hurry, Brother Turkey?'

'I am going down to the big town, Brother Anansi.'

'Why are you going to the town?' asked Anansi.

'Oh, Brother Anansi, I must go to the barber's for a hair-cut now and then.'

Br'er Anansi looked at Turkey's bald head in surprise. To think of poor, silly, old bald-headed Turkey talking about barbers and hair-cuts and having his hair cut! He laughed and laughed until his sides hurt him, and he said:

'Brother Turkey, how can you be so stupid? Where will you get hair to be cut and brushed?'

Turkey turned red and said: 'It's all right, Mr. Anansi, never mind about my hair. If you don't give back the fowls and goats and corn that you took from Tiger and Goat and the others, the Old Hag will come for you tonight! And if she doesn't come, we will all be there, Brother Anansi, and perhaps that will be worse so you'd better be quick!' That is how it came about that Anansi gave back all the things he had taken from his neighbours, just because of Turkey's bald head.

And that is the reason why nobody ever laughs at Turkey's bald head.

ANANSI AND TURTLE
AND PIGEON

TURTLE once lived next door to Pigeon, and across the road
was Anansi's house. Sometimes Turtle and Anansi would
stand together and watch Pigeon flying from one house-top to
another, from one tree to another.

'I wish I could fly with Pigeon,' said Turtle.

'I wish so, too,' said Anansi.

At last one day they went to Pigeon and asked him to teach
them to fly. Pigeon took them to the oldest pigeon of all. He
looked as wise as an owl and said that they could learn. Then
each pigeon pulled out a feather and glued it to Turtle's back
until he looked like a pincushion, all full of feathers. Anansi,
they said, would have to let Turtle try first. Next they took
hold of Turtle and flew up into the air.

Soon they reached Tiger's cornfield. Every day the pigeons
went there and took Tiger's corn. When they got there they
took their feathers away from Turtle, gave him a large bag,
and told him to pick up the grains of corn from the ground. So
they all picked up corn; and Turtle picked up corn, too.

Then they heard a noise.

The pigeons all stood still and lifted up their heads. A
second or two later the oldest pigeon flapped his wings and
rose up, and all the other pigeons flapped their wings and flew
away, leaving Turtle all by himself in the field of corn. Anansi
saw the pigeons return home, but there was no Turtle with
them. Turtle was left in the middle of the field, and there the
watchman found him with the bag of corn.

'So it's you, Turtle, is it? You are the thief that comes and steals Tiger's corn?'

'No,' cried Turtle, 'no, my sweet watchman. Ask Anansi if you doubt me. It is the pigeons that come stealing the corn.'

'What are you doing here, then?' asked the watchman.

'Oh, my sweet watchman,' cried Turtle, 'ask Anansi if you doubt me. I told the pigeons that I wanted to fly, and they lent me feathers and I came with them; but I am not stealing the corn.'

'Well,' said the watchman, 'I never yet saw a turtle fly. You must come with me.' And he put Turtle in a pail of water and took him to Tiger's house.

Now Turtle remembered what Anansi had once told him.

Anansi once said: 'Turtle, when you don't know what to say and when you don't know what to do—sing!' So Turtle began to sing. He sang so sweetly that the watchman began to dance, and he danced until he had spilled all the water out of the pail. Then Turtle called out, 'If you let me walk I will sing so sweetly!'

But the watchman said no.

At last they came to Tiger's house, and Tiger came out to see Turtle.

'Ah,' said Tiger, 'call the cook!' Tiger told the cook how to stew Turtle for supper, and then he went off to invite his relations and friends to come to the meal.

Now the cook was mixing all the onions and pimento together, and Turtle remembered what Anansi had said, and Turtle began to sing. He sang so sweetly that the cook began to dance.

Then Turtle said, 'My sweet cook, if you will only put me on the ground outside I will sing so sweetly!'

The cook put Turtle outside, and he sang more sweetly than ever; and the cook danced all the time.

Then Turtle said: 'Oh, my sweet cook, if you will take me to the river and put just the tip of my tail in the water I will sing more sweetly than ever.'

The cook took Turtle to the river and put just the tip of his tail in the water, and Turtle sang more sweetly than ever, and the cook danced and danced.

But soon she heard no singing. She looked down.

There was Turtle at the bottom of the river! And Turtle waved his hand and swam away.

And the cook dared not go back to Tiger's house.

That is why, from that day to this, no one cooks Tiger's food for him.

KISANDER

KISANDER was a cat.

Anansi and Mouse were afraid of Kisander. She could see in the dark. She could walk so swiftly and so softly that no one knew when she was coming. Anansi and Mouse (whose full name was Mouse Atoo and whose pet name was Moos-Moos Atoo) feared Kisander's sharp teeth and cruel claws and her eyes that shone bright in the dark.

But Kisander had a dokanoo tree, and the tree had lovely puddings on it. No one else had such a tree. Anansi and Moos-Moos both loved the puddings, and whenever they went past Kisander's garden they wondered how they could get some of the puddings from Kisander's tree.

Kisander was very proud of the tree. In the mornings she would go out and take a hoe and dig round the roots of the tree until she had made a little gutter. Then she filled the gutter with water, and this made the puddings grow large and sweet.

One evening Mouse Atoo was talking with Brother Anansi.

Anansi said: 'Did you see the dokanoo tree in Kisander's garden, Mr. Moos-Moos Atoo?'

'Yes,' said Moos-Moos, 'and do you know, Brother Anansi, I would like to lay my hands on some of the lovely puddings on that tree. They are ready for picking now. My mouth waters every time I think of them.'

'And mine, too, Mr. Moos-Moos Atoo. Whenever I pass by Kisander's house I go very quickly and very quietly, but last evening the puddings seemed so lovely that I had to stop and look at them. Couldn't we creep into Kisander's yard and pick some, Brother Moos-Moos Atoo?'

Anansi and Moos-Moos whispered together. Later that night, at about nine o'clock, Anansi and Moos-Moos Atoo stole out of their houses. No one was looking. Quietly they crossed over the gully and crossed the field. Then they crawled under the hedge and so got into Kisander's garden.

There was the dokanoo tree. They could see its shape in the darkness, and Anansi whispered:

'Moos-Moos, I tell you what I will do. I will go up the tree and knock off the puddings. You must stay at the bottom of the tree. Watch carefully. If you hear that old Kisander come out you must call to me.'

So Moos-Moos stayed at the bottom of the tree while Anansi climbed up to the branches where the puddings grew. His eyes had become accustomed to the darkness of the night, and he could make out the puddings very clearly. When he looked down he could see his friend Moos-Moos turning his head this way and that, on the look-out for Kisander.

Slowly and carefully Anansi crawled out on to a branch. Here was a pudding hanging all ripe and ready. He drew his knife and cut the stem. The dokanoo fell 'boof' on the ground. Moos-Moos and Anansi waited breathlessly, without a sound.

Kisander, asleep in bed, was awakened by the sound and said: 'What's happening to my dokanoos? They are falling off the tree in the night. The breeze must be stronger than when I went to bed.' Then she turned over and went to sleep again.

Brother Anansi crawled further along the branch. Here was another lovely pudding, all ripe and ready. Quickly he drew his knife and cut the stem that held the pudding to the tree.

'Boof,' the pudding fell to the ground.

Kisander turned over in her bed. 'What is happening to my dokanoos?' she said. 'They are falling off by themselves in the night. They must be getting too ripe.' Then she turned over and went back to sleep.

Anansi and Moos-Moos breathed again. That last 'boof' had been very heavy, but no one in the house had stirred. Kisander was a sound sleeper. They only had two dokanoos. It was worth while trying to get a third.

Anansi crawled further out along the branch. He drew his knife and cut a third dokanoo. This was an even heavier one. It fell 'boof' to the ground; and this time Kisander got out of bed saying, 'I must go out and see what is happening to my puddings.'

So Kisander came to the door of the house, opened it, and looked out. Kisander's eyes shone in the dark. Moos-Moos heard the door open, and he saw the two eyes shining in the darkness. He must warn Anansi; but he dared not use Anansi's name, since Kisander would hear and would find out who was picking the puddings. I will call him Ceiling Thomas, thought Moos-Moos quickly to himself, because he is a spider and walks on the ceiling. And so he called out:

'Kisander, Kisander,
Sing Atoo, Atoo, Atoo, sing Atoo.
Ceiling Thomas, run oh!
Ceiling Thomas, run oh!
Ceiling Thomas, I am going to run oh!'

In a flash Moos-Moos was through the hedge and away while Kisander came running out towards the dokanoo tree. She looked here and there and all around. No, there was nothing but three dokanoos lying where they had fallen on the ground.

'I must get a lantern to see what is the matter,' said Kisander. She hurried away and in a minute or two came back with a storm lantern. She looked everywhere but could see nothing except the three dokanoos on the ground. She walked round the tree. There were only the three dokanoos on the ground. Kisander said:

'Hi! This is the first time that I have ever seen dokanoos fall off a tree all by themselves, and with their stems cut by a knife!'

Anansi was still up in the tree, hiding behind the leaves. When Kisander went back into the house with the dokanoos, he jumped from the tree—'boof'—and ran away as fast as he could. Kisander hurried back into the garden and looked all around. No, there was no other dokanoo on the ground. 'That's funny,' said Kisander.

She never found out what had made that last 'boof.'

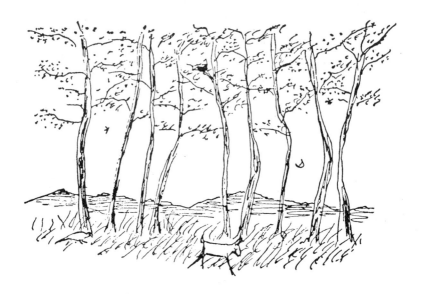

THE KLING KLING
BIRD

In the days when Anansi and Tiger were still friends, a very
long time ago, there was a bird that everyone called the Kling
Kling bird. It built its nest on the top of the slender bamboo
trees. In the evening, when the breeze came down from the
mountains, the slender bamboo trees waved to and fro, up and
down, and rocked the Kling Kling bird to sleep.

Anansi was friendly with the Kling Kling bird. Many a time
he sat and watched the bird building its nest where the evening
breeze would rock it gently to and fro. Many a time Anansi and
the bird played cards together before the hour came for the
breeze to blow and for the bird to go to bed.

'You know, Mr. Kling Kling, it's easy to beat you at cards,'
said Anansi while they were talking together one evening just
before bedtime.

'Easy to beat me! You mean easy to be beaten by me,' said
Kling Kling quickly. 'Haven't I just won the game?'

'That's just once in a while,' said Anansi.

'I'll tell you what we will do,' replied Kling Kling. 'We will make a bargain. Tomorrow the one who loses must pay a fine to the one who wins, and the fine is this: the one who wins may take a piece of flesh from the one who loses.'

Anansi agreed. Day after day he lost the game, and the Kling Kling bird took so much flesh away from him that Anansi became very thin. Finally his patience gave out. He said that he would play only one game more. They played one more game. This time Anansi won. Full of delight he cried out, 'Now then, Brother Kling Kling, I am going to take a piece of flesh from you.' Anansi was so pleased that he laughed. At last his turn had come.

But the Kling Kling bird said 'Why?' and flew away.

For a long time Anansi tried to catch Kling Kling. They were friends no longer. Anansi set traps and hid them in the grass near the berries on which Kling Kling loved to feed. He made the withes from the woods into long, slippery nooses and hid them where Kling Kling liked to walk. But it was no use. Kling Kling was too clever. He saw all the traps and avoided them. Sometimes he would hide in the top of a tree and, without a sound, watch Anansi set a trap; then when it was all done he would suddenly cry out 'Why?' and fly away, leaving Anansi puzzled and angry.

At last Anansi went to his friend Tiger, and said:

'I beg you, Mr. Tiger, help me to catch that old Kling Kling bird. He wouldn't pay his fine. He flew away, and I cannot catch him at all.'

'And what will you give me if I help you catch him?' asked Tiger.

'Oh, my sweet Tiger,' said Anansi, 'I will give you a cow.'

'A whole cow?' asked Tiger, who was very greedy and very fond of cow.

'A whole cow, Mr. Tiger. I promise,' said Anansi. So Tiger thought and thought for a long time and at last he said:

'I tell you what we will do, Br'er Anansi. I will lie down in the house and pretend to be dead. You must take a bell and walk all round the town calling out at the top of your voice: "The great King Tiger is dead; the great King Tiger is dead."

Then all the people will come to the funeral, and you can catch him.'

Now the next day was a great market day. Kling Kling went to the market and bought peas and rice and codfish and plantain and sweet potatoes. While he was buying the sweet potatoes he heard a bell ringing, and he asked the people what it was. 'Ah,' said a stout market-woman, 'the great King Tiger is dead.'

'What! You mean that Tiger, the great Tiger, is dead?' asked Kling Kling.

'Yes,' said the people standing round; 'yes, what she says is true. The great King Tiger is dead.'

'And when did he die?' asked Kling Kling.

'Yesterday just before twelve o'clock.'

'Then,' cried Kling Kling, 'I must hurry away to put on my second-best coat and go to the funeral.' Kling Kling rushed home and put on his second-best two-tailed blue coat and his shoes that were so new that they cried out 'quee-quee' when he walked in them. When he had finished dressing Kling Kling went to Tiger's house. When he got there he saw a great crowd of people outside, and he shook his head and said:

'So the great King Tiger is dead!'

'Yes,' they replied, 'the great King Tiger is dead.'

'When did he die?'

'Yesterday just before twelve,' they replied.

'What killed him? Was it fever? Was it an accident? How did he die?'

'The heat of the weather killed him,' they said.

'And has he laughed at all since he died?' asked Kling Kling. 'No.'

'Then he isn't dead at all,' said Kling Kling. 'Don't you know that a man is not dead until he laughs a big last laugh?'

Tiger was in the nearest room, listening at the window. When he heard what Kling Kling said he broke out into a great laugh that shook the house, and Kling Kling said, 'Ha-ha, I never yet heard a dead man laugh!' and he flew away. So Tiger never got the cow.

BANDALEE

WHISPERS went through the forest.

Whenever two of the forest creatures met they put their heads together and whispered. Even those that usually kept far apart could be seen whispering in each other's ears—even Tiger and Goat, Mongoose and Chicken, Dog and Cat were busy whispering to each other.

It was all about Land Turtle. They whispered to each other that Land Turtle had become a very rich man.

Anansi heard the whispers. He believed that they were true, and he made up his mind that he would get some of Land Turtle's money. His eyes shone when he heard of all the money that Land Turtle had. Surely it would not be hard to trick Land Turtle, who looked so slow and stupid.

'I never knew that Land Turtle was so rich,' said Anansi to himself. 'I thought he was a poor man. He hasn't any sense either, so he has no right to be rich. I've never seen anyone move as slowly as Land Turtle, except Brother Worm. It won't be hard to take some of his money from him.'

Anansi crawled under his bed and pulled out from the darkest corner an old calabash that he used to hide his savings. Slowly he counted it, and the counting did not take long because there was so little money. 'I must get to work,' said Anansi, and he set off for the bank. He lodged his money in the bank and then went to Land Turtle's house.

Now it happened that Land Turtle was a much wiser creature than he seemed. He moved slowly, but he could think fast. When he saw Anansi coming he guessed that there was some reason for the visit, and so he told his wife and children to hide themselves while he talked with Anansi.

'Good morning, Brother Land Turtle,' said Mr. Anansi,

who was a little breathless because he had walked so fast. 'It's a long time since we two met.'

Land Turtle bowed but said nothing.

'It's a long time since I paid you a friendly visit,' said Anansi.

Land Turtle bowed again, but said nothing.

'Yes, a long time,' said Anansi. 'To tell you the truth, you would not have seen me today at all; but I went for a long walk, and, as I was tired, I turned in here on my way home to rest a while. Yes, I went to the bank to put in some money because if we do not save we will never have anything.'

'That is true,' said Land Turtle, who was still wondering why Anansi had come.

'You know, Land Turtle,' said Anansi, 'perhaps we could make a bargain. You have money in the bank. I have money in the bank. I want more, and you want more. Now suppose we agree to run a race to the bank. The one that wins will get all the money belonging to the two of us.'

Land Turtle was silent for a few minutes. He saw through Anansi's scheme.

'That's not fair, Anansi,' he said. 'Look how fast you walk and how slow I am. You'd get to the bank long before me. But I'll agree to race you if you promise you will run as a spider, and not change yourself into a man.' It was well known that Anansi could change himself whenever he wished.

'I'll agree to run the race as a spider,' Anansi said.

He knew that even in his spider form, running along his rope, he could run faster than Land Turtle. What a fool Land Turtle is, thought Anansi, to dream of racing me.

'Well, Brother Anansi,' said Land Turtle, 'since we have made the bargain, the next thing is to decide where we shall start from. As you know, there are two roads that lead to the bank.'

'Pshaw,' said Anansi, 'a road is a road. One is just as long as the other. We can talk about that tomorrow. Let's go to the bank and tell the banker that the one of us that gets there first tomorrow is to have the money, yours and mine put together.'

So they went to the bank and explained it all to the banker,

38

and then they went home to get a good night's sleep. Land
Turtle called his wife and his sons and his daughters, and told
them about the race. 'Anansi is very cunning,' he said, 'but this
time Land Turtle is going to be cunning, too. But I will need
your help.' And then he told them what they must do.

Now Land Turtle knew that Anansi would suggest that each
should go by a different road. One road followed the river, and
another ran up on the bank a little way. Every little while, there
was a crossing that joined the two. Early in the morning of the
day of the race, Mr. Land Turtle and his children walked along
the river road; and wherever there was a crossing, one of the
children sat down to wait. For old Brother Land Turtle and
his children looked so much alike that nobody could tell one
from another. Mr. Land Turtle's oldest son went to meet
Anansi at the starting-place, and Mr. Land Turtle himself took
up his station at the last crossroads. As soon as he was sure that
the race had begun, he planned to run to the bank, get all the
money, and go back home through the woods.

All the animals had come out to see the race. Some stood at
the starting-place, some waited outside the bank. Soon Anansi
came along, all smiles and confidence. He could almost feel the
weight of Land Turtle's money in his pocket.

Stupid old Land Turtle. Look at him, thought Anansi, as he looked at what he thought was Mr. Land Turtle, but what was in fact Mr. Land Turtle's oldest son.

Just as Land Turtle had thought, Anansi suggested that they run by different roads and call out to each other from time to time. Land Turtle's son nodded his head, to show that he agreed; and Anansi called out—one, two, three—and away they went. Soon Anansi was well ahead of Land Turtle, yet when he came to the first crossing and called out, 'You Turtle, you Turtle,' he heard a voice reply: 'Anansi oh, Anansi oh, bandalee, bandalee.'

'Well,' thought Anansi, 'Land Turtle isn't far behind.' And he ran faster. At the next crossing he called out again,

'You Turtle, you Turtle,' and one of Land Turtle's children answered: 'Anansi oh, Anansi oh, bandalee, bandalee.'

'I never thought Land Turtle could run so fast,' said Anansi to himself. 'I must run faster if I'm to get the gold.' And away he went.

Once again at the third crossing Anansi called out, 'You Turtle, you Turtle,' And once again one of Land Turtle's children called out, 'Anansi oh, Anansi oh, bandalee, bandalee.'

'Faster still, faster still,' thought Anansi to himself. He began to feel anxious. By the time he got to the last crossing he hardly had enough breath to call out, 'You Turtle, you Turtle.'

This time no answer came.

'At last,' said Anansi to himself, 'at last I am well ahead. Now for the money at the bank.' But at that very moment Land Turtle was leaving the bank with his own money and with the few pence that belonged to Anansi.

Anansi was sure that he had left Land Turtle far behind, so he slowed down and walked into the bank as if he owned it.

He asked for his money and Land Turtle's, but the banker told him that he had already given the money to Land Turtle.

'What,' panted Anansi, 'do you mean that Land Turtle got here first?'

'Yes,' said the banker. 'Land Turtle came in fifteen minutes ago.'

'Are you sure that it was Land Turtle?' asked Anansi.

'Quite sure,' said the banker. 'I know Land Turtle well, and I gave him the money.'

Out rushed Anansi as fast as his legs could carry him. In the distance he could see Land Turtle toiling along.

'To think that slowcoach beat me in a race,' cried Anansi. 'Stop, Turtle, stop.'

Land Turtle did not stop, but Anansi soon caught up with him.

'So you won the race,' said Anansi. 'Well, well, who could have thought it? Let us walk home together.'

Poor Land Turtle was very frightened. However, Anansi was so friendly that soon Land Turtle was calm again. Quietly they walked along until they came to a pond. Anansi saw his chance.

'Let's both dive in,' he said, 'and see who can stay under the water longest.'

Land Turtle was pleased to see how well Anansi had taken his defeat, and he readily agreed. Besides that, he was proud of his diving. This was the one thing in which he felt certain that he could beat Anansi every time. He put down his bag of gold at the edge of the pond, and both Anansi and Land Turtle dived in at the same time.

Land Turtle stayed under for as long as he possibly could. Surely Anansi would lose for the second time in one day. Then he came up but, alas, both Anansi and the money had gone.

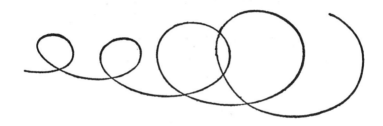

YUNG-KYUNG-PYUNG

ACROSS the river, on the side of the forest furthest from Anansi's village, there lived a king who had three daughters. No one in the world knew their names. Wise men had come from many far-off lands to guess the names, but they had all failed.

Even wise old Owl had failed. He had gone across, and he had spent a long time looking at the King's three daughters. Then he had returned without saying a word. It was clear that Owl did not know what the names were.

Even wise old Mr. Goat had tried and failed. When he came back home he told Mr. Anansi about his visit. In the end Goat had only been able to say, 'Beah! Beah!' in disgust. The King had laughed at him. 'Go away, Mr. Goat,' he had shouted. 'I would never think of calling a child of mine "Beah".' Goat had tried to explain that this was only his favourite exclamation, but all the court was laughing so loud that no one even heard what he was saying.

'Well, Br'er Goat,' said Anansi, 'perhaps I had better go

45

and find out the names of those girls. No one can do it better than I can.' So Anansi set off for the King's court.

The following day the three girls went down to the river to swim. While they were away Anansi found a pretty basket and filled it with flowers and fruit. He put in it some juicy-looking mangoes and oranges, some bananas and pawpaw. Around the rim of the basket he put some yellow flowers of the alamanda and white blossoms from the oleander. Then he took the basket, placed it in the middle of the eldest girl's room, and hid under the bed.

About half an hour later Anansi heard laughter and merry voices. The girls had come back from the river. No one else was with them. As soon as they came into the room the eldest girl cried out,

'Yung-Kyung-Pyung! What a pretty basket!
Marg'ret-Powell-Alone! What a pretty basket!'

The next girl sang in reply,

'Marg'ret-Powell-Alone! What a pretty basket!
Eggie-Law! What a pretty basket!'

Then the youngest said,

'Eggie-Law! What a pretty basket!
Yung-Kyung-Pyung! What a pretty basket!'

Then they took up the basket and ran to show it to the King. Anansi heard it all. Quickly and quietly he crept from underneath the bed, stole out of the room, and hurried away from the palace. He went to his own home and got together a little band of musicians. There was Rat with his drum, Crow with his fiddle, Bullfrog with his trumpet. He spent a week teaching his band the tune that he wanted them to play.

'Why are you doing all this?' asked Rat. 'And when will we be paid? Have you any money?'

'None now,' said Anansi, 'but I promise you all the money you want by Saturday.'

On Saturday Anansi set off with his band. They went down the forest road, crossed the river, and went to the King's palace. As they drew near the palace, Anansi said, 'It's time to play, now. Play the tune, and I will sing the words.'

So they played, and Anansi sang at the top of his voice, 'Yung-Kyung-Pyung, Eggie-Law, Marg'ret-Powell-Alone!'

After they had repeated the tune some six times, the Queen called out and asked, 'Who is calling the names of my daughters?'

'Play louder,' cried Anansi, and they all marched into the palace singing and playing, 'Yung-Kyung-Pyung! Eggie-Law! Marg'ret-Powell-Alone!'

The King heard the voices and called out, 'Who is calling the names of my daughters?'

Then Anansi marched into the King's room with his band. 'You, Anansi!' shouted the King. 'I should have known it would be you. Take what you wish from my palace, but be out of the country within an hour and never come back.'

Anansi and his men did not need to be told twice. Crow filled his beak with gold; Bullfrog took all the silver he could carry; and Anansi put so much gold and silver into his bag that he could not lift it, but had to pull it along the ground.

But Rat was cleverest of all. He took the King's eldest daughter, Yung-Kyung-Pyung, and married her. He stayed in the King's palace. The King agreed to the wedding, but he made Rat promise never to play the drum again.

ANANSI AND
THE PLANTAINS

IT was market day, but Anansi had no money. He sat at the
door of his cottage and watched Tiger and Kisander the cat,
Dog and Goat, and a host of others hurrying to the market to
buy and sell. He had nothing to sell, for he had not done any
work in his field. How was he to find food for his wife Crooky
and for the children? Above all, how was he to find food for
himself?

Soon Crooky came to the door and spoke to him. 'You must
go out now, Anansi, and find something for us to eat. We have nothing for lunch, nothing for dinner, and tomorrow is Sunday.
What are we going to do without a scrap of food in the house?'

'I am going out to work for some food,' said Anansi. 'Do not
worry. Every day you have seen me go with nothing and come
home with something. You watch and see!'

Anansi walked about until noon and found nothing, so he
lay down to sleep under the shade of a large mango tree. There
he slept and waited until the sun began to go down. Then, in
the cool of the evening, he set off for home. He walked slowly,

for he was ashamed to be going home empty-handed. He was asking himself what he was to do, and where he would find food for the children, when he came face to face with his old friend Rat going home with a large bunch of plantains on his head. The bunch was so big and heavy that Brother Rat had to bend down almost to the earth to carry it.

Anansi's eyes shone when he saw the plantains, and he stopped to speak to his friend Rat.

'How are you, my friend Rat? I haven't seen you for a very long time.'

'Oh, I am staggering along, staggering along,' said Rat. 'And how are you—and the family?'

Anansi put on his longest face, so long that his chin almost touched his toes. He groaned and shook his head. 'Ah, Brother Rat,' he said, 'times are hard, times are very hard. I can hardly find a thing to eat from one day to the next.' At this tears came into his eyes, and he went on:

'I walked all yesterday. I have been walking all today and I haven't found a yam or a plantain.' He glanced for a moment at the large bunch of plantains. 'Ah, Br'er Rat, the children will have nothing but water for supper tonight.'

'I am sorry to hear that,' said Rat; 'very sorry indeed. I know how I would feel if I had to go home to my wife and children without any food.'

'Without even a plantain,' said Anansi, and again he looked for a moment at the plantains.

Br'er Rat looked at the bunch of plantains, too. He put it on the ground and looked at it in silence.

Anansi said nothing, but he moved toward the plantains. They drew him like a magnet. He could not take his eyes away from them, except for an occasional quick glance at Rat's face. Rat said nothing. Anansi said nothing. They both looked at the plantains.

Then at last Anansi spoke. 'My friend,' he said, 'what a lovely bunch of plantains! Where did you get it in these hard times?'

'It's all that I had left in my field, Anansi. This bunch must last until the peas are ready, and they are not ready yet.'

'But they will be ready soon,' said Anansi, 'they will be ready soon. Brother Rat, give me one or two of the plantains. The children have eaten nothing, and they have only water for supper.'

'All right, Anansi,' said Rat. 'Just wait a minute.'

Rat counted all the plantains carefully and then said, 'Well, perhaps, Br'er Anansi, perhaps!' Then he counted them again and finally he broke off the four smallest plantains and gave them to Anansi.

'Thank you,' said Anansi, 'thank you, my good friend. But, Rat, it's four plantains; and there are five of us in the family—my wife, the three children, and myself.'

Rat took no notice of this. He only said, 'Help me to put this bunch of plantains on my head, Br'er Anansi, and do not try to break off any more.'

So Anansi had to help Rat to put the bunch of plantains

back on his head. Rat went off, walking slowly because of the weight of the bunch. Then Anansi set off for his home. He could walk quickly because the four plantains were not a heavy burden. When he got to his home he handed the four plantains to Crooky, his wife, and told her to roast them. He went outside and sat down in the shade of the mango tree until Crooky called out to say that the plantains were ready.

Anansi went back inside. There were the four plantains, nicely roasted. He took up one and gave it to the girl. He gave one each to the two boys. He gave the last and biggest plantain to his wife. After that he sat down empty-handed and very, very sad-looking, and his wife said to him, 'Don't you want some of the plantains?'

'No,' said Anansi, with a deep sigh. 'There are only enough for four of us. I'm hungry, too, because I haven't had anything to eat; but there are just enough for you.'

The little child asked, 'Aren't you hungry, Papa?'

'Yes, my child, I am hungry, but you are too little. You cannot find food for yourselves. It's better for me to remain hungry as long as your stomachs are filled.'

'No, Papa,' shouted the children, 'you must have half of my plantain.' They all broke their plantains in two, and each one gave Anansi a half. When Crooky saw what was happening she gave Anansi half of her plantain, too. So, in the end, Anansi got more than anyone, just as usual.

ANANSI AND
FISH COUNTRY

THERE was famine in the land. For months there had been no rain. Day after day the sun rose and set in a cloudless sky. The grass changed from green to yellow to parched brown. The parched leaves of the trees cried out for water. The plants in the fields withered away. There was famine in the land.

Anansi was hungry. He felt as if he had been hungry for weeks, for months, for ever. Now he must go off to some other place to find food.

'If I only had a bag and a long coat,' he said to himself, 'I would go to Fish Country and pretend to be a doctor. That's it,' he thought to himself; 'the only thing that a doctor wants is a black bag and a long coat and a long face.'

No sooner said than done! By next morning Mr. Anansi had his tall hat and black bag and long coat. Then he set off. When Anansi got to Fish Country he took an office and outside it he put up a signboard: 'M. Anansi, Surgeon.'

The first patient was a very large, fat fish. She had many children and grandchildren and great-grandchildren. Now her eyes were troubling her. Could Mr. Anansi help her?

Anansi looked at her eyes from every angle. He spent a long time looking, and as he looked he talked to himself. Sometimes he shook his head or stopped and coughed as he had seen doctors do. He seemed to be thinking hard. At last he said, 'Yes. Your eyes are very weak, but I think that I can help you. Will you do what I tell you?'

'Yes, doctor, I will,' said the fat old fish, who was now very frightened.

'Very well,' said Anansi. 'Go to bed as soon as you get home. See that your maid makes up a big fire in your room and puts a frying-pan beside it, along with some coconut oil and a sharp knife. Call me when you are ready.'

The fat fish hurried home as fast as she could and told the maid to make a fire. Soon everything was ready, and she sent to call Anansi.

As soon as Anansi came to the house he said to the relatives: 'All of you must leave the room. I will lock the door. Do not try to look inside, but listen carefully. When you hear the frying-pan say "fee-fee" you must all stamp on the floor and sing this song:

"Bim, Bam, my grannie's eyes are well, oh,
Bim, Bam, my grannie's eyes are well, oh,
Bim, Bam, my grannie's eyes are well, oh,
Make a lot of noise."'

Quickly the fishes learned the tune and the words. When Anansi was satisfied that they could sing the song without his help he went into the room. First he locked the door, and then he put the frying-pan on the fire and put the oil in the pan. As the oil got hotter the frying-pan sizzled and called out 'fee-fee.' Quickly Anansi put the fat fish in the frying-pan while outside all the other silly fish sang as loudly as they could: 'Bim, Bam . . .'

And while they sang Anansi ate the fish. When he was no longer hungry, he began to think about getting away. But what was he to do? Quietly he put all the bones and scales in the bed and wiped his mouth with the sheet so that no crumbs showed; and then he covered the bones with the sheet. He took up his bag, put on his longest face, opened the door, and faced the crowd of fishes.

'All is well,' he said. 'The operation was very successful. Leave the fish alone for two hours. You have been making a lot of noise, but now you must be still. Now you must pay me my fee.'

The fish paid Anansi the money he requested, and away he went. He meant to leave Fish Country as quickly as possible.

There was a river to be crossed, however, and when Anansi came to the river he was horrified to find that it was full of alligators. How was he to get across?

Just at the moment Anansi saw Brother Dog on the other side of the river.

'Ah, Brother Dog,' he cried, 'are you glad to see me?'

'No,' barked Dog.

'Ah, but you would be glad if you knew how much money I have here,' said Anansi, shaking the bag of money.

'Bring it,' barked Dog.

'But I must cross the river!' said Anansi.

'Cross now,' barked Dog.

'The alligators will eat me,' cried Anansi. 'Look how hungry they are.'

'Leave that to me,' barked Dog. He began to run along the bank, away from Anansi, barking as he went. The greedy alligators followed him, thinking that he was going to jump into the water. And while they chased Dog, Anansi dashed across the ford and was soon safe on the other side. He knew that

Dog was stronger than he was, and so he left the bag of money by the ford. Dog was very pleased with himself.

When the fish came to the bank of the river, which was the boundary of their kingdom, they saw Anansi. But what could they do? He was running through the forest singing,

'Bim, Bam . . .'

TICKY-PICKY
BOOM-BOOM

At last the famine was over. The rains came. First heavy black clouds covered the sky, and then the rain came down in floods. The dry earth seemed to drink up the rain until it could drink no more. The parched brown grass became green. Life started again, and everyone began to plant.

Even Anansi set to work. Never before had he worked so hard or so long. At last the large square of land round his house was full of yams and potatoes.

Now the yams were ready. Anansi looked out from his

window at the field of yams and said to himself: 'I must have a garden with flowers in it, like a rich man. I will get Tiger to come and dig up the yams for me.'

Anansi went to Tiger and said: 'Good morning, Mr. Tiger. I hope you are very well. I beg you to come with your hoe and machete and dig my yams.'

'What will you give me?' asked Tiger, stroking his moustache and looking hard at Anansi. He was beginning to be a little suspicious of this Anansi, who always got the better of him.

'I will give you all the yams that you dig up,' said Anansi.

That was fair enough, thought greedy Mr. Tiger. Next morning he went to Mr. Anansi's house early with his hoe and machete; and he dug and dug; and the more he dug, the more the yams seemed to grow down into the ground. By and by four o'clock came, working time was over, and Tiger had not dug up a single yam.

Tiger was angry. He looked at the yams and the deep holes that he had dug round them, and he thought of how hard and long he had worked, and he could keep his temper no longer. Tiger took his machete and chopped at one of the yams with it. He chopped into little pieces as much of the yam as he could reach, and then he set off for home.

What was that? There was a noise behind him. Tiger looked round, and he saw all the yams coming after him.

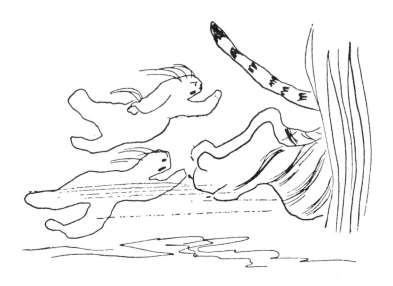

Some of the yams had one leg, some had two legs, some had three legs, some had four legs.

And the noise that their feet made as they came stamping and running down the road sounded like this:

'Ticky-Picky Boom-Boom,
Ticky-Picky Boom-Boom, Boof!'

Tiger began to run. The yams ran, too. Tiger began to gallop. The yams galloped, too. Tiger jumped. The yams jumped. Tiger made for Brother Dog's house as fast as he could, and he called out at the top of his voice:

'Oh, Brother Dog, Brother Dog, hide me from the yams.'

Dog said, 'All right, Tiger, hide behind me and don't say a word.'

So Tiger hid behind Dog.

Down the road came the yams, stamping on their two legs, three legs, four legs:

'Ticky-Picky Boom-Boom,
Ticky-Picky Boom-Boom, Boof!'

And they said, 'Brother Dog, did Tiger go this way?'

Mr. Dog looked straight ahead and said: 'You know, Mr Yam, I can't see Mr. Tiger at all.'

But Tiger could not keep still. He was so frightened that
he called out, 'Don't tell them, Mr. Dog!' And Mr. Dog was
so angry that he ran away and left Tiger.

And the yams jumped.

And Tiger jumped.

And the yams ran, and Tiger ran.

The yams galloped, and Tiger galloped.

Then Tiger saw Sister Duck and all the little ducklings by
the side of the river. Tiger hurried to her as fast as he could
and cried, 'Sister Duck, hide me, hide me from the yams that
are coming.'

'All right, Tiger,' she said. 'Get behind me, but don't say
a word.'

So Tiger hid behind Sister Duck.

By and by the yams came stamping along.

> 'Ticky-Picky Boom-Boom,
> Ticky-Picky Boom-Boom, Boof!'

And the yams said: 'Sister Duck, have you seen Tiger?'

Sister Duck looked straight ahead and said: 'I can't see him,
Yams, I can't see him at all.'

But Tiger was so frightened that he called out, 'Don't tell them, Sister Duck, don't tell them!' And Sister Duck was so angry that she moved away and left him to the yams.

And the yams jumped, and Tiger jumped.

And the yams ran, and Tiger ran.

And the yams galloped, and Tiger galloped.

Tiger was growing tired. Always he could hear the yams coming behind him. At last he came to a little stream, and over it there was a plank of wood. On the other side was Mr. Goat.

Tiger ran across the plank as fast as he could and he cried: 'Oh, my Brother Goat, hide me from the yams that are coming.'

'All right, Tiger, but you must not say a word.'

So Tiger hid behind Goat.

The yams came stamping down the road:

'Ticky-Picky Boom-Boom,
Ticky-Picky Boom-Boom, Boof!'

When they reached the little bridge they called out, 'Mr.Goat, have you seen Tiger?'

Mr. Goat looked straight ahead, but before he could say a word Tiger called out, 'Don't tell them, Mr. Goat, don't tell them!'

The yams jumped on to the wooden plank and tried to cross; but Goat put his head down and butted them, one after another, so that they all fell into the river and were broken in pieces.

Brother Tiger and Brother Goat picked up all the pieces and went off to Tiger's home to have a great feast.

And they never asked Anansi to the feast of yams.

And sometimes, when the night is dark, Tiger still feels frightened when he hears someone stamping down the forest track with a noise that sounds like:

'Ticky-Picky Boom-Boom,
Ticky-Picky Boom-Boom, Boof!'

ANANSI AND
THE ALLIGATOR EGGS

ANANSI curled himself up and went to sleep under the shade
of the breadfruit tree. It was much too hot for work. Only a
foolish man would work when it's so hot, he said to himself.

Now, as he lay there half asleep, he heard some birds talking to one another. They were at the top of the tree, but by
listening carefully he could just catch the words. He could
hear a Blue Quit say:

'The dokanoos are ripe now. Yesterday I flew past the tree,
and I could see that some of them are almost ready to fall from
the tree.'

'Dokanoos!' At the mention of the word Anansi was wide
awake. He remembered the dokanoos that Moos-Moos and
he had tried to take from Kisander's tree. Was there another
tree laden with dokanoos?

'Yes,' said another Blue Quit. 'We had better go across to
the trees tomorrow before anyone else finds out where they
are.'

When Anansi heard this he opened his eyes and called out
softly: 'Brother Bird, Brother Bird, I hear you talking about
dokanoos. Tell me about them, Mr. Blue Quit.'

'It's no use your troubling your head about these dokanoos,'
laughed the bird. 'It's a big, big tree that we are talking about;

but you would never be able to get to it because it stands on a little rock in the middle of a big river. You could never get to it without flying.'

Br'er Anansi's face fell. He thought for a moment, and then he said, 'Is that true, Brother Blue Quit? Oh, what a pity it is that I never learned to fly.' At this all the birds, even the tiny grey Grass Quits, began to laugh so much that Anansi cried out:

'I bet you that I could learn to fly as well as any of you if only I had a few feathers to make wings.'

The birds laughed louder than ever, and one of the Blue Quits said: 'All right, Br'er Anansi, if you can learn to fly you can come with us. If each one of us gives you a feather you will have enough to make wings—but, remember, if you fall into the river it's your own fault; and, remember, the river is full of alligators.'

Brother Anansi had a great respect for alligators. The thought of those sharp teeth, those jaws that opened so wide, kept him back for a while—but then there was the taste of the dokanoos! No, he must take the risk; and so he said:

'Fair is fair, Mr. Blue Quit. Each of you give me a feather and then watch me fly as high as Chicken Hawk.'

Each bird pulled out a feather and handed it to Anansi. He took some of the whitish, sticky gum that comes from the

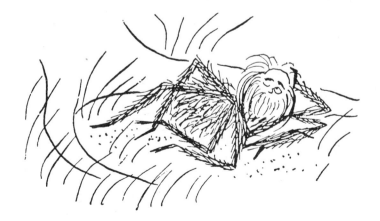

breadfruit tree, and with it he fastened the feathers to his two
shoulders. When he was finished he had a fine pair of wings.
There on Anansi's shoulders were the small grey feathers of
the Grass Quit, the longer blue-grey feathers of the Blue Quit,
the white-edged feathers of the White Wing. The birds
laughed for they had never seen wings made in such a fashion
or with so many different feathers. They laughed still louder
when Anansi climbed up to the top of a post, jumped off, and
fell to the ground. After two or three falls Anansi learned to
flap his new wings, and he called out: 'I can fly now as well
as you. Take me with you tomorrow. I can fly, Brother Bird;
and before long I will be singing as well as Brother Nightin-
gale, too! Take me with you, Brother Bird.'

What could they do? The birds agreed to meet Br'er Anansi
at the breadfruit tree early the next day.

When morning came Anansi went to the tree even before
the birds began to open their eyes and sing their morning
prayers. He waited until he heard them, and then he called
out: 'Good morning, Brother Bird! aren't you all ready
yet?'

'Yes, Anansi, we are all ready. Come, we are going this way.'
Then they all flew off to the big river with Br'er Anansi in the
midst of them, flapping his wings with the best. As they flew
over the river Anansi looked down, and he almost fell with

fright. Never had he seen so wide a river. How full of alligators it must be.

But just then a bird called out, 'See the tree, Brother Anansi! See it there on the rock in the middle of the river!' They all flew as fast as they could. 'I saw the tree first. I have first choice,' Anansi shouted. He had forgotten all about the alligators.

The birds flew to the tree and began to feed, but Brother Anansi kept pushing them out of the way. One of the Blue Quits had just begun to eat a dokanoo when Anansi pushed him aside, saying, 'You can't do that, I saw it first.' The Blue Quits were all angry at this and they said, 'If we had known that it was going to be like this we would have left you where you were.'

'And if it comes to that, give me back my feather,' said one of the Blue Quits that had been pushed aside.

'Feather!' cried Anansi. 'What is a feather? A dokanoo is what I want. You can't eat feathers!'

At this all the birds pounced upon Anansi and every one pulled out the feather it had given him. Then they all flapped their wings and flew away from the tree, leaving Anansi on the branch of the tree with his mouth full of dokanoo.

Evening came, and Br'er Anansi could eat no more. He filled his bag and climbed down from the tree. He had no feathers, no wings. The birds had gone. What was he to do?

He made up his mind to wait at the foot of the tree until morning. The birds would come back then, and he would ask their pardon and beg for the feathers. But next day no birds came. He ate as many dokanoos as he wished, but as the day passed he grew more and more anxious. At last he said to himself, I had better come down from this tree and see if I can swim across the river.

When Anansi reached the bank of the river he took up a small, dry stick and threw it into the water. It floated. 'That's easy,' he said. 'If a stick can float, I can float, too; for I am better than a stick.' Just then he caught sight of Br'er Alligator, who had gone down into the water for a swim. He called

out, 'Br'er Alligator, come and help me.' He was terrified of Alligator, but he dared not stay any longer on the island. Perhaps there was some way in which he could persuade Alligator to help him.

'Who is that?' shouted Alligator.

'It's Anansi,' he called out. 'It's your cousin Anansi. I can't swim across, Brother Alligator. Carry me on your back across the river.'

Alligator swam up to where Anansi was standing and said, 'Come, get on my back, Anansi.'

There was nothing else to do. Trembling with fear, Anansi climbed on to Alligator's back—how tough and ugly it was! After he had swum a little way, Alligator said, 'Now I will take you to see my home, Anansi.'

'Th-th-thank you, my friend Mr. Alligator,' stammered Anansi. 'I want to see your home.'

When they had reached Alligator's house on the steep side of the island, Alligator asked Anansi what had happened. Anansi told how the birds had left him, but he did not tell the reason; and then he said, 'And, Mr. Alligator, when I saw you I knew that you would help me, for I am your cousin; and I picked this bagful of dokanoos for you.'

'Thank you, Brother Anansi,' said Alligator. 'I am glad to get the dokanoos because I like them but cannot climb the trees to pick them. It's a shame that the birds left you. Because you have brought the dokanoos for me, and because we have had dealings before, I won't eat you this time; but perhaps next time, Br'er Anansi, perhaps next time . . .'

Alligator laughed, and Anansi could do nothing but stare at his mouth, full of sharp teeth.

Now Brother Alligator had twelve eggs, and every morning and every evening he took the eggs to the river, washed them clean, and put them back in the room. 'You stay with me till evening,' said Alligator, 'and I will get someone to take you across the river. Now come and help me wash the eggs.' He took Anansi into the room and showed him the eggs. Anansi's eyes nearly fell out of his head when he saw them. He looked at his empty bag but said nothing. He helped Alligator pick up the basket of eggs and carry them out to the river's bank. Then he said, as he thought of his empty bag:

'You wash them, Brother Alligator. I shall stand behind you and pass them to you from the basket one at a time, and I'll put them back when they have been washed.'

The minute that Br'er Alligator turned his back Br'er Anansi put the first egg into his mouth and ate it quickly. Then he passed an egg to Brother Alligator and sang out, 'One.'

'One,' called Brother Alligator.

'Two,' said Br'er Anansi.

'Two,' answered Brother Alligator.

'Three,' said Br'er Anansi.

'Three,' counted Brother Alligator.

So Anansi counted and so he ate, counted and ate, until he

had eaten eleven of the twelve eggs. For all this time it was the same egg he passed to Brother Alligator. Every time it was handed to him clean he rubbed it in the mud and passed it back again. When at last he had counted twelve, he called out: 'All right, Brother Alligator, I'll carry the basket back to the house while you wash your hands.' He put the one lone egg in the basket and took it back to the room, and Brother Alligator didn't know what had happened.

Then Alligator called his son and said to him: 'Get the boat and find Jack Fish and King Fish. Tell them to row Anansi across the river to his home.' Soon the boat was ready, with Jack Fish and King Fish in their places, and they set off with Anansi.

When the boat had almost reached the far shore, Alligator happened to go into his room, and there he saw the basket with only one egg in it. He knew what had happened. He called out at the top of his voice:

'Jack Fish, oh! King Fish, oh! Bring back Anansi!'

But it was too late. The boat had touched shore, and Anansi jumped out and disappeared into the forest before Jack Fish and King Fish could hear the voice of Alligator from a far distance across the water. That's why, to this day, Anansi keeps away from alligators.

ANANSI AND
THE CRABS

ONE day Anansi took it into his head that he would like to go preaching. But he could not find anyone who would listen to him. The animals had their own preachers; the crows had a preaching crow and the birds had a preacher bird. No one wished to listen to Anansi.

Anansi was very sorry about this. He wanted to dress himself up in a long black gown and preach, but he could not find anyone who would listen to him. That was a pity. Reverend Crow looked fine in his long black gown. When he preached, all the other crows gathered round him and listened. Anansi wished that he could find someone who wanted him as a preacher.

Then one day Anansi heard that the crabs had no preacher. They had no church. So Anansi bought a long black preacher's gown and went off to Crab Town on Sunday morning. There was no church for the crabs, but there was a big tree which would serve as shelter. Anansi stood under the tree and began to preach. He preached and he preached, but not a crab came out to listen to him. They all stayed at home and slept. Anansi preached so long and so loud that he became hoarse. It was no use. The crabs slept on. Sadly he took off his long black gown and went back home.

Next Sunday morning Anansi set off for Crab Town again. This time he passed by Rat's house. Rat was standing at the door of his house, so Anansi stopped to say good-morning.

'And where are you going so early?' asked Rat, taking his pipe out of his mouth.

'I am going to church, Mr. Rat. Will you come with me?'

'I might as well,' said Rat. He put on his tall hat and his long-tailed coat, which he always wore when he went to church, and went off with Anansi.

Anansi told Rat how he had preached for a long, long time and very loud the Sunday before, and how no one had come to listen to him. Then he said:

'Mr. Rat, I am glad that you have come with me. When these crabs see a fine gentleman like you listening to me they will be sure to come and listen, too.'

When they reached Crab Town, Anansi and Rat went to the big tree. Rat sat down quietly while Anansi put on his new black preacher's gown and began to preach. He preached longer and louder than ever. Every now and then Rat nodded his head to show that he agreed. But not a crab came out. The crabs slept on.

'Can you understand it, Rat?' asked Anansi as they walked home together. 'You heard how long I preached, and how loud. You nodded your head again and again. What can we do to make the crabs come out?'

'I'll tell you what we will do,' said Rat. 'I think we should bring one or two other people. I will ask Crow and Bullfrog to come with us next week.'

The following Sunday all four friends set off for Crab Town. Anansi preached longer and louder than ever. Rat nodded his head so much that it nearly fell off. Crow called out 'Amen' every two minutes. Bullfrog gurgled 'Hallelujah.' It was a wonderful service, but no crabs came to listen. They just stayed at home and slept.

On the way back all four were silent, until Crow said, 'I wonder if they would like it better if we had some music?'

'I am sure that you are right,' said Rat. 'You bring your fiddle, Crow; and I will bring my big drum, and Bullfrog will bring his trumpet.'

Sunday came, and the friends set out once more for Crab Town with their instruments. They took their places under the big tree, and started to play.

The crabs heard the music and wondered what was happening. They sent a young crab to find out. The young crab saw Rat banging away at his big drum, 'boom, boom, boom.' John Crow fiddled away as fast as he could, so that his fiddle went 'squea, squea, squeak!' Bullfrog blew out his chest until it was twice as big as usual, and his trumpet sounded 'baw, baw, baw.' The crab listened, and then Anansi began to preach. The music seemed to be finished, so the young crab went back to his home and told the others what he had seen and heard. The crabs went back to sleep.

Anansi saw that he would have to do something still better. He asked his friends if they would allow him to baptize them in the river, and they agreed. On the following Sunday they all put on long white gowns and went to Crab Town. They marched in line, singing loudly. Rat sang tenor, while Crow and Bullfrog sang a deep loud bass. Anansi led the way to the river, and he dipped them each three times in the water—first Rat, then Crow, then Bullfrog!

When the crabs saw the baptizing they wanted to join in the fun. They hurried along to the river. 'Anansi! Anansi!' they cried. 'We want to be baptized.'

76

This was what Anansi and Rat and Crow and Bullfrog were all waiting for. 'Go put on your long white robes and come back,' they said. 'Then we'll baptize you.'

Back came the crabs in their long white gowns. Down to the river they went, four by four. Anansi, Rat, Crow, and Bullfrog took the crabs and dipped them into the river—once, twice, and three times; and then they clapped them into the big sack they had handy to take them home for dinner, for they were all very fond of crab. When the bag was full, Anansi called out, 'That's all the baptizing for today'; and he and his friends started off home.

'What wonderful preaching,' said Anansi. 'We'll go back next Sunday and preach some more.'

Now on Monday morning the great King of the Crabs heard how Anansi had taken the crabs away by a trick, and he went to see his friend Alligator and made a complaint against Anansi. Alligator agreed that Anansi had no right to take crabs that way, and he promised to tell Anansi that it must never happen again. So Crab King went back to his home, and Alligator sent a message to Anansi that he wished to see him.

Anansi was afraid of Alligator. He was strong, and had long sharp teeth, and was not a person to trifle with. Anansi knew he had to go, so he put on a long face and went to Alligator's home by the river as fast as he could.

'Good morning, Cousin Alligator,' he said. 'How are you today?'

'What do you mean, "Cousin"?' asked Alligator. 'I didn't know you were my cousin.'

'Oh, yes,' said Anansi, 'your father and my mother were first cousins. Didn't you know that? My mother used to say, "You never need fear Alligator, because he's your cousin."'

Alligator thought about this. 'Well,' he said, 'all of us alligators can drink boiling water. If you're my cousin, you've got to prove it by drinking boiling water.'

'That I shall do, Cousin Alligator,' said Anansi. 'Pour out the water for me to drink, and I'll prove it to you.'

Alligator poured some boiling water out of the kettle into a pan and gave the pan to Anansi. Anansi lifted the pan to his mouth and pretended to drink it. 'This water isn't hot enough,' he said. 'I'll put it out in the sun to make it hotter.'

Alligator thought that was a good idea. So Anansi sat the pan in the sun until it had cooled off, and then he drank it.

'Now you see, I've drunk the boiling water, Cousin Alligator.'

'So you have. So you have. And I never knew we were cousins. Well, I'll keep my promise not to trouble you.'

So Anansi went home. But he didn't do any more preaching.

THE QUARREL

In the beginning Anansi, Tiger, and Monkey were friends.
They rented some land down by the river and set about clearing it. Every morning they went off to work, talking and laughing. Anansi talked more than the others. He carried the
lunch-box. He liked his lunch very much indeed.

Here was the field. Monkey and Tiger set to work at once.
Anansi rested in the shade of the mango tree for a while. Then
he went out and worked with his friends for a little. Then he
went back to the shade of the tree to see that the lunch was
safe. Then he worked a little more. Then he rested a little
more. When lunch-time came Tiger and Monkey were very
tired, but Anansi was very fresh.

When the field had been cleared, the friends planted Indian
corn in it. In the mornings they would go out to see how the
young plants were growing. The plants grew quickly and soon
began to bear. Before long the corn in the ears was full. It was
time to reap the corn.

One morning Monkey, Tiger, and Anansi were in the field
looking at the fine crop of corn. Suddenly Monkey called out.

'Look,' he cried, 'look there. Someone has been breaking the corn. Someone has been stealing our corn!'

Tiger and Anansi looked. It was true. The corn had been reaped in one part of the field. How angry they were! Anansi seemed the angriest of all. He seemed to be so angry that Monkey began to wonder. He knew Anansi well. Could it be that Anansi himself had taken the corn?

Monkey told Tiger what he thought. They decided to watch the field without telling Anansi.

When night came, Monkey and Tiger went to the field. Monkey climbed the mango tree and sat out on a branch. Tiger sat by the fence and watched. There was a full moon, so both Tiger and Monkey could easily see what was happening.

One hour passed, and then another. All was quiet. This is very dull, thought Tiger.

Another hour passed. It was twelve o'clock. Time for bed, said Monkey to himself, rubbing his eyes.

What was that? Down by the southern fence something was moving. There was no wind, but in that part of the field the leaves were bending as if a wind were blowing over them.

Monkey looked carefully. He was quite sure that someone was there. He decided to climb down from the tree quietly, warn Tiger, and then catch the thief.

Monkey jumped down from the branch to the ground. It was an easy jump for him, and no one would have heard him if he had not jumped on to a dry stick that lay on the ground. It broke with a noise like a pistol shot. The noise frightened the thief. Both Monkey and Tiger heard the sound of running feet, and they followed as quickly as they could. Out of the field they ran, then across the road and in among the trees. The sound of footsteps became clearer. They were gaining on the thief. Now they could see him as he ran across a stretch of open ground. It was Anansi.

Monkey and Tiger were very angry. They ran all the more quickly. Anansi could see that they would soon catch up with him. Besides, he was already growing tired.

Suddenly Anansi saw a grain of corn on the path. 'Help me,' he cried. 'Hide me, hide me, grain of corn.'

The grain of corn opened and then closed again. There was Anansi hidden inside the grain of corn. Monkey and Tiger ran past. They did not see the grain of corn. They could not find Anansi.

Before long it was morning. As the sun rose, Mr. Rooster flew down from his perch and set off down the path to the river. He was hungry and thirsty. Ah, there on the path in front of him was a grain of corn. He swallowed it quickly. There was Anansi inside the grain of corn inside Mr. Rooster.

Mr. Rooster stood by the bank of the river. He did not see someone who was very hungry. He did not see Mr. Alligator until it was too late. And now there was Mr. Anansi inside Mr. Rooster inside Mr. Alligator.

All this time Monkey and Tiger were looking for Anansi. They looked here, they looked there, but they could not find him.

'I tell you what we will do,' said Monkey at last. 'We'll ask our oracle drum.'

'Yes, the oracle drum will tell us if we beat it in the right way,' said Tiger.

Monkey and Tiger placed the oracle drum carefully on the ground. They stood, one on each side, and began to beat the drum.

> 'One, two and three, four,
> Tell me what is true,
> Tell me what is true,
> One and two and one and twenty,
> Where in the world is old Anansi?'

They stopped and the drum gave back these words:

> 'One and two and one and twenty,
> This will lead you to Anansi.
> By the river lives a strong one;
> Open him and find a rooster,

Open him and find a grain,
And within the grain, Anansi.'

At first Monkey and Tiger could not believe this. We have made a mistake, they thought. But the oracle drum said the same thing every time they tried.

'Well, let us try,' said Tiger. Down by the river they found the strong one, Mr. Alligator. They cut him open. Inside was the rooster, just as the oracle drum had said.

'Cut open the rooster,' shouted Monkey.

They cut open the rooster. There was the grain of corn, just as the oracle drum had said.

'Cut open the grain of corn,' shouted Monkey, 'and I will catch Anansi as he jumps out.'

They cut open the grain of corn, but Anansi was too quick for them. Like a flash he was off down the road. Tiger and Monkey followed fast behind him.

Again Anansi could see that they were gaining on him. As he passed a banana tree he called out, 'Banana tree, banana tree, help me.'

The banana tree gave Anansi one of its strong fibres. He took the fibre and quickly climbed an orange tree near by. Monkey and Tiger were catching up with him. He tied the fibre to a branch, and then he swung with the loose end to a near-by branch. To this he tied the other end, so that the fibre hung like a bridge between the two branches.

Monkey was climbing the tree. Soon he would be on the branch. Anansi climbed out to the middle of the fibre and waited.

The fibre was too weak to carry Monkey. Anansi sat out in the middle of the fibre and laughed at Monkey.

'Come, Monkey,' he mocked, 'come and catch me.'

Tiger looked up. 'Just stay there, Monkey,' he said. 'Do not move. He will soon want something to eat.'

Before long Anansi began to feel hungry. He felt hungrier than ever when Monkey said, 'Look, Tiger, you go and have your breakfast. When you come back I will go and have mine.'

Tiger came back half an hour later, smiling and licking his lips. Then Monkey went off while Tiger watched. Half an hour later Monkey came back, smiling and licking his lips. How hungry Anansi felt!

'Ah, there is a fly,' thought Anansi. 'If I go down, Tiger and Monkey will catch me. If I stay here, perhaps I can find a way of catching the fly, and that will be food enough for me.' Slowly Anansi began to add another thread and then another to the fibre, until at last he made a web . . . and in the web was the fly.

That is why Anansi the spider lives in a web.

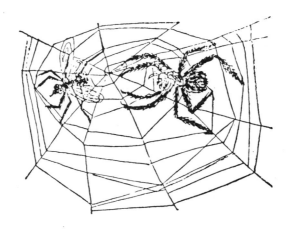